A WOODLAND MYSTERY ™

The Haunted Halloween

A WOODLAND MYSTERY
By Irene Schultz

To Isabel Gutierrez, my dear and brave friend

The Haunted Halloween
©1996 Wright Group Publishing, Inc.
©1996 Story by Irene Schultz
Cover and cameo illustrations by Taylor Bruce
Interior illustrations by Meredith Yasui
Map illustration by Alicia Kramer

Woodland Mysteries™
© Wright Group Publishing, Inc.

The Woodland Mysteries were created by the
Wright Group development team.

The Wright Group
19201 120th Avenue NE
Bothell, WA 98011

Printed in the United States of America

10 9 8 7 6 5

ISBN: 0-7802-7225-0

What family solves mysteries...has adventures all over the world...and loves oatmeal cookies?

It's the Woodlanders!

Sammy Westburg (10 years old)
His sister Kathy Westburg (13)
His brother Bill Westburg (14)
His best friend Dave Briggs (16)
His best grown-up friend Mrs. Tandy
And Mop, their little dog!

The children all lost their parents, but with Mrs. Tandy have made their own family.

Why are they called the Woodlanders? Because they live in a big house in the Bluff Lake woods. On Woodland Street!

Together they find fun, mystery, and adventure. What are they up to now?

Read on!

Meet the Woodlanders!

Sammy Westburg
Sammy is a ten-year-old wonder! He's big for his fifth-grade class, and big-mouthed, too. He has wild hair and makes awful spider faces. Even so, you can't help liking him.

Bill Westburg
Bill, fourteen, is friendly and strong, and only one inch taller than his brother Sammy. He loves Sammy, but pokes him to make him be quiet! He's in junior high.

Kathy Westburg
Kathy, thirteen, is small, shy, and smart. She wants to be a doctor some day! She loves to be with Dave, and her brothers kid her about it. She's in junior high, too.

Dave Briggs

Dave, sixteen, is tall and blond. He can't walk, so he uses a wheelchair and drives a special car. He likes coaching high-school sports, solving mysteries, and reading. And Kathy!

Mrs. Tandy

Sometimes the kids call her Mrs. T. She's Becky Tandy, their tall, thin, caring friend. She's always ready for a new adventure, and for making cookies!

Mop

Mop is the family's little tan dog. Sometimes they have to leave him behind with friends. But he'd much rather be running after Sammy.

Table of Contents

Chapter 1: The Great Idea

"Hey, Sammy! Sammy! Listen!"

Fourteen-year-old Bill Westburg raced through the kitchen door.

His brother Sammy, ten, was looking

out the kitchen window.

He said, "Bill, you really missed it! Kathy left half a peanut butter sandwich on a plate out there." He pointed to the yard.

"She had to come in for the phone.

"And you know that fat old blue jay we named Pig? Well, he flew down and took the whole sandwich!

"He could hardly get up off the ground with it.

"He went flap ... flap ... flap... but finally he ... "

Bill said, "Sammy, forget that bird! Listen to my great idea! Let's have a haunted house here for Halloween! What do you say?"

Sammy said, "I say I think your brain's out to lunch, that's what I say. There's ALREADY a haunted house every year in your school basement.

"And EVERYbody goes to it."

Bill nodded. "That's the point! I just heard that a water pipe broke at school. It flooded the basement. And Halloween is tomorrow night!"

Sammy said, "Why didn't you say so in the first place? Let's have a haunted house here! Gosh, I'm so glad I thought of the whole idea."

Just then, their sister Kathy, thirteen, came in. Sixteen-year-old Dave followed in his wheelchair.

Mrs. Tandy was with them.

The five of them, best friends, lived together. They called themselves the Woodlanders.

Mrs. Tandy said, "What's this about a haunted house?"

Sammy said, "I have this perfectly great idea! Well, Bill might have helped me think of it … "

Bill broke in. "Sammy, someday you're going to push me too far."

Sammy just stuck out his tongue.

Bill went on. "Anyway, Bluff Lake Junior High can't have our haunted house this year.

"Broken water pipe. I thought it would be fun to have a haunted house here."

Mrs. Tandy said, "It would be!

"Everybody loves Halloween. Even the high-school kids go trick-or-treating."

4

Dave said, "We could make the basement into a ghost walk ... and put scary things all over the place."

Bill nodded. "And I was thinking of a scavenger hunt, too."

Sammy said, "SCAV-en-jer? What's scavenger?"

Bill said, "It's where you make up a list of strange things. Then everyone tries to find them."

Dave said, "Hey, could we ask people to bring a little money ... for UNICEF?

"You know, the United Nations Children's Fund? My school's collecting for it."

Kathy looked at Dave shyly. "But some kids might not have any extra money."

Bill said, "Well, we can say that anyone can come ... and that we only want them to give money if they can."

5

Sammy jumped up out of his chair. "Stop talking about money, Bill! We have to talk about important things! Witches! Bats! Ghosts! Haystacks!"

Mrs. Tandy said, "What about pumpkin faces … and black cats?"

Dave added, "Don't forget spiders! And goblins!"

Bill looked at Sammy. "Speaking of goblins, what's that you're gobbling, Sammy?"

Sammy slid the last blob of chocolate pudding into his mouth.

Bill said, "Wait a minute! Isn't that MY chocolate pudding that I saved from dinner last night?"

Sammy said, "Hey, that reminds me, what kind of food should we make for our Halloween haunted house?"

Now Bill looked mad. "DON'T CHANGE THE SUBJECT, SAMMY!

"I told you YESTERDAY I was saving my chocolate pudding for today!"

Sammy stuck out his chocolate-coated tongue at Bill.

It was the LAST STRAW! Bill made a dive for Sammy.

Sammy dived under the table. He almost landed on Mop. Mop started to bark.

Then Sammy crawled out from under the table near the kitchen door.

He ran outside. He yelled in, "Calm down, Bill!

"I'll make you more dumb old chocolate pudding!

"Anyway, it wasn't very good. It had lumps in it. You aren't such a great cook, you know."

That did it! Bill EXPLODED!

He raced after Sammy.

Sammy yelled,

"Can't catch a housefly,

Can't catch a flea,

Can't catch a baby and you

Can't catch ME!"

Then he ran around to the front door, and inside to his room.

He locked the door just as Bill started banging on it.

He dived into his closet and began digging in the corner.

At last he found what he was looking for. He pulled it over his face. It was a gorilla mask.

Bill yelled, "Open up this door, you brat!"

Sammy heard how mad Bill sounded. He began to feel sorry about eating the pudding. After all, most of the time Bill was his best pal.

He called through his door, "OK, OK, I'm sorry. If I open my door, will you promise not to kill me?

"You're older, so you should be nice to me ... even if I'm almost as big."

Bill couldn't help smiling at that.

9

He said, "OK, I'm not so mad anymore. Open up."

Sammy said, "All right. I have a surprise."

He un-locked the door. Bill opened it.

There stood Sammy, the gorilla.

The gorilla grunted and scratched his stomach.

He banged his fists on his chest.

He said, "Gorilla help Bill.

"Good gorilla never steal chocolate pudding again."

Bill ended up laughing.

He said, "OK, gorilla. Let's go plan our Halloween house."

Chapter 2:
Trouble on the Street

They hurried back to the kitchen.

Dave said, "Let's write down what we have to do.

"Let's see ... fix up the basement ...

invite neighbors ... make the lists for the scavenger hunt ... "

Sammy, still in his gorilla mask, added, "Food ... and costumes."

Kathy got into the swing of things. "Let's fix up the front woods so it's really scary out there.

"You know, ghosts hanging from trees ... strange noises."

Sammy broke in. "I can make the strange noises with my clarinet. I can make the strangest noises you've ever heard!"

Bill laughed. "We know, we know. We've all heard you practice.

"You're in charge of awful noises all right!"

Sammy went to his bedroom and got his tape recorder.

Just then a really awful howling noise started up in the woods.

12

Dave said, "That's the coon dog ... you know, Howler, from down the street.

"He must have gotten loose again. Now THAT'S a strange noise!"

Sammy jumped up. He grabbed his tape recorder and ran outside.

When he returned he was still in his gorilla mask. "I've got some Halloween noises already. Wait till you hear them! They're great!"

He played the tape and explained, "Here are some branches breaking. Howler's owner did it, running through the woods.

"And there's Howler, howling."

Then the tape gave a blood-curdling scream.

Sammy said, "And that's Howler's owner ... when he saw me break through the woods right next to him. I forgot I still had on my gorilla mask!"

13

Bill laughed. "Well, gorilla, let's get on with our plans."

Mrs. Tandy said, "What do you think of giving out popcorn balls for trick-or-treats?"

Bill said, "Great! Maybe we can make them tonight."

Sammy took off the mask and laid it on the table.

Dave said, "Are you using that mask this Halloween, Sammy?"

Sammy said, "No, I was a gorilla last year. Everyone would guess who was inside it if I wore it again."

Mrs. Tandy said, "Well now, do you want to lend the mask out? I wouldn't mind being a gorilla this year.

"I could put black socks on my arms and legs. And wear a black turtleneck shirt, and my regular clothes."

Sammy said, "And you're tall enough.

You'd be a much better gorilla than almost anyone else!"

Mrs. Tandy laughed. "Gee, thanks a
lot, honey. That's the WORST nice thing
anyone has ever said about me."

Dave said, "Well, let's see, back to the
food plans. What drink should we serve?"

Sammy said, "Well, I know what we SHOULDN'T serve. Grape juice. It shows forever on your clothes when you spill it.

"How about lemonade?"

Dave said, "Lemonade sounds good to me. And cookies."

Then Mrs. Tandy asked, "How many people should we invite?"

Kathy said, "About fifty. That's not too many.

"No one will stay long. They'll take a quick walk-through and want to be outside."

Sammy jumped up and said, "I can just see how it'll be!

"First they'll come to the basement and get their PANTS scared off!"

"Then we will calm them down with some lemonade and cookies."

He made his voice sound slow and deep. "Then we will send them out to their DOOM!"

He half-closed his eyes, like a lizard.

He wrapped his fingers around his own neck.

He gasped, "They'll go off into the black night, scavenger hunting and trick-or-treating ... "

He dropped to his knees.

"And vampires will get them!"

Then the great actor, Sammy Westburg, fell flat on the kitchen floor. He lay on his back as if he were dead.

Everyone clapped.

He jumped up and bowed.

Then Bill said, "Hey, we have to make invitations."

Dave nodded. "And we have to be sure to collect them at the door ... so no one comes who isn't invited."

Kathy said, "Let's have people use the basement door. That'll keep all the mess down in the basement. We can put that on our invitations!"

Just then they heard a car door slam. Sammy ran outside. He came back leading John Hemster, the police chief of Bluff Lake.

Sammy said, "I brought you a present, Mrs. T. ... your BOYfriend."

The chief said, "Speaking of boyfriends, I saw some boy walking with that cute little King girl today. The boy sure looked a lot like you, Sammy."

Sammy didn't say another word about boyfriends.

The chief went on. "I'm here to tell you there's been more trouble on your street.

"You know about that burglary two weeks ago?

"Well, now someone has cut a hole in a basement window. Could have been a burglar. And it happened only two houses down from you.

"Whoever it was got scared away, but be on guard.

"And be sure to lock your doors with dead bolts. Burglars have trouble breaking in past them."

As he finished his last sentence, the phone began to ring.

Sammy ran to answer it.

He came back and said, "I could hear breathing, but no one said anything."

Mrs. Tandy said, "That's funny. That's the third time today!"

Dave shook his head. "It's not so funny. Burglars do that sometimes, to find out if anyone's home!"

Chapter 3:
Big Halloween Plans

Chief Hemster said, "Police cars will keep checking this street.

"And I'm adding an officer on foot, in plain clothes.

"You know her. Officer Rita Sanchez. She will be around tomorrow."

Bill said, "Can you come to our haunted house tomorrow night? It's in our basement."

The chief smiled. "I'll be on duty, but I'll sure try to drop in.

"Good-bye for now!"

They waved as he let himself out.

Kathy pushed a piece of paper across the table to the others. "Look! I've been working on the invitation."

She had written this:

Come to our Haunted House!
Enter through the
Woodlanders' basement door!
Saturday, Halloween
6:00 - 7:00 pm.
Cookies, lemonade, monsters!
Bring money for UNICEF
if you can.
Bring this invitation to get in!
Scavenger hunt: 7:15 - 8:15 pm.

Dave smiled at Kathy. "That's good!"

Sammy said, "Good? What do you mean, good? That's way too much for us to write on fifty invitations!"

Bill said, "Calm down. We can take them to the copy place."

Sammy said, "Oh ... then it's OK. Hey, why don't I cut out a bunch of black haunted houses? We can paste the invitations right onto them!

"A great idea! I'm a genius!"

Bill said, "All right, genius. Listen to your genius brother—I know how to make the basement really scary.

"First we tear rags in thin strips, and hang them from the ceiling.

"We can keep wetting them down, so they'll flop against people's faces and feel terrible!"

Sammy said, "Perfect! And we can cook up some big noodles ... and chill

23

them till they feel cold and dead.

"Then we add something sour to them, like vinegar.

"Then we tell people they're worms ... and we make everyone eat one in the dark to get out!"

Sammy gave a horrible little laugh. He added noodles to the list.

Dave said, "How about bobbing for apples? And what if we have a maze ... you know, that you have to find your way out of.

"They had one once in the junior-high haunted house.

"They moved desks together and made a twisting path to follow."

Kathy said, "Let's make our basement pathway with a rope!

"People would have to hold it and follow it in the dark!"

Dave said, "Let's see. We could say

they have to follow it to get to the cookies and lemonade."

Bill said, "GREAT! First it can lead into the basement bedroom. We could put something scary in there."

Sammy said, "I've got it! Light flashing on our cardboard skeleton!"

Dave said, "We could get some special paint for the skeleton ... the kind that glows in the dark!

"Then we wouldn't even need to shine a light on it.

"And we can paint other stuff with it, too."

Kathy grinned. "We could even paint the maze rope!

"Then we could lead it through a thousand spiderwebs!"

Dave said, "Sure! We can hang threads from the ceiling for webs."

Sammy smiled a creepy smile.

25

He said, "Everyone would have to crawl through them. ICK! It'll be great!"

Mrs. Tandy said, "We could use some old sheets to divide off the basement."

Kathy added, "And we could cut out horrible creatures and pin them to the sheets. They'd make scary shadows!"

Sammy said, "That's good! With a little practice you could be a really mean kid!"

Mrs. Tandy said, "If that's your idea of a compliment, Sammy, I'd hate to hear your insults." Then she mussed his hair and hugged him.

She added, "Well, what are we sitting here for?

"Add rope to the list, Dave. And glow paint. And let's go shopping!"

Sammy shouted, "Race you to Dave's car, Bill!"

. . .

As they ran to the garage, a gray car drove slowly past the house. Only Kathy noticed it.

Four doors.

Dent in the rear fender.

Two thin men in the front seat wearing sunglasses, the kind that look like silver mirrors.

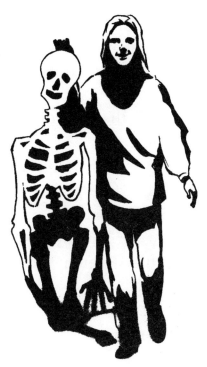

Chapter 4:
The Basement of Fear

They shopped and rushed home.

Mrs. Tandy said, "You get started without me. I want to start turning out cookies for tomorrow. I'll come down to

29

the basement in a while."

The others started right in on the basement.

Kathy brought the old cardboard skeleton from upstairs.

Dave spread newspapers. They painted over the white parts of the skeleton with their glow paint.

They turned off the lights to look at it. There lay the skeleton, glowing in the dark.

Sammy gasped, "It's wonderful! Now I know what I'm going to make for my costume! A skeleton!

"I'll paint bones on a black leaf bag and wear it.

"And I have an old skeleton mask ... well, I mean Bill does. You'll let me wear it, won't you, Bill, old pal, my best big brother?"

Bill grinned at Sammy's fishy sweetness

But he nodded yes.

Sammy ran upstairs. He came down carrying a huge black bag. He was wearing the skeleton mask.

Bill said, "Sammy! You knew right where to get that mask! I bet you go through my drawers when I'm out!"

Sammy pretended he didn't hear.

He turned to Kathy and said, "Kathy, you've got to help me.

"Paint me a skeleton on both sides of this bag."

31

Kathy said, "I bet you can do it yourself, Sammy. Start copying the cardboard skeleton. I'll help."

He painted as she pointed ... backbone ... ribs ... shoulder blades ... hips ... leg bones ... arm bones ... bones for hands and feet.

At last Sammy said, "I'll paint the other side when this dries.

"Right now I'll show you a GREAT decoration I invented in school today. My teacher really HATED it!"

He cut off the foot from an old black sock. He filled it with newspaper. He tied it closed with heavy black yarn. He tied yarn around the toe.

It looked like a black bump sticking off of a black lump.

He held it in the air. He said, "It's perfect! It's disgusting!"

Kathy asked, "What is it?"

Sammy said, "It's a SPIDER'S BODY! This bump is the head!"

He added eight pipe-cleaner legs.

Then he dipped the legs into black paint.

He and Kathy made six more big spiders and hung them around.

Then Mrs. Tandy came down. She and Dave and Bill began to lay out the rope for the maze.

First they tied it to the arm of the couch near the back door ... then to a chair in the basement bedroom.

Bill said, "Take it across the bed to that hook on the wall. Everyone will have to crawl over the bed."

Then they took it out the bedroom door ...

over to an old dresser
back and forth between chairs
over to the leg of the big table
under the table to a cot
into the laundry room
past the laundry sinks
through the walk-through closet
into the workshop

... and at last they tied it to a post near the food table.

Dave said, "Wow! It's seven already! There's still so much to do before tomorrow night! I hate to stop to make dinner."

So he and Kathy went out to get some pizzas.

After eating, they started back to work.

They all cut monster shapes out of newspaper.

Mrs. Tandy and Bill hung the wall of sheets.

Dave and Kathy pinned the monsters on.

Bill set a lamp on the table. The light shined through the sheets.

Sammy shouted, "The shadows are HID-EE-US! Really hideous!"

By then it was 9:00!

Mrs. Tandy said, "I've baked three triple recipes of cookies, but I think we may need more.

"I think I'll mix up another triple batch tonight."

Kathy said, "Let's finish the whole basement tonight, too.

"Then we can spend tomorrow on our costumes ... and the woods ... and the popcorn balls ... and the invitations."

35

Sammy was all for it. "It'll be twelve o'clock before we finish. I LOVE staying up late!"

So Mrs. Tandy went up and mixed another triple batch of oatmeal cookies.

Bill and Sammy and Kathy tore rags into strips.

Dave decided where to put them, and the others tacked them to the ceiling.

Bill said, "Here's how we keep them wet." He held a pail of water up to dip each strip.

Sammy said, "Let me do that! I can do it better than you."

He grabbed at the pail. SPLOSH! Some of the water dumped on his head.

He said, "Bill, you did that on PURPOSE! I'm going to ... "

In the middle of the sentence a buzzer went off in the kitchen.

Mrs. Tandy yelled, "Come on up, cookie testers! I'm taking the last batch out!"

Kathy and Sammy raced up the stairs.

Bill and Dave zoomed up the outside ramp.

They all flopped down in the kitchen to eat some cookies.

Sammy said, "Before, I thought I'd want to work all night. Now I'd give anything to flop into bed!"

Mrs. Tandy said, "Me, too. What do you say we call it a day? We can finish the rest tomorrow."

So they went off to bed.

■   ■   ■

And they didn't see the four-door gray car with the dent in its rear fender.

It drove slowly around and around the neighborhood.

37

Chapter 5: Officer Sanchez

Morning.

Saturday morning.

Halloween morning!

Everyone but Kathy was in the kitchen.

Sammy said, "What are we having for breakfast?"

Mrs. Tandy asked, "Who's got a good idea?"

Dave said, "How about French toast? I'll make it."

Bill said, "I'll help."

He took out half a dozen eggs.

He broke them into a bowl, laying the shells on the counter.

Sammy watched him like a hawk. He LOVED to catch Bill in a mistake.

Then he looked into the bowl. "Hah, look! You dropped a little piece of shell in there. Ick!"

Then he grabbed half an eggshell from the counter. He used it like a spoon to lift out the little piece.

He bragged, "Mrs. T. taught me that. She knew I'd need to rescue us from your cooking someday, Bill."

Bill just laughed, and poured a glass of milk into the eggs.

Dave beat in a little salt. Then he dropped some bread slices into it. He looked around. "Where's Kathy?"

Bill said, "I'll go see."

But Kathy came running in.

She said, "I've been watching out my window. I saw something funny."

Dave said, "What, Kathy?"

Kathy said, "Come look out the dining-room window with me. Maybe they'll drive by again."

But they saw nothing but the woods and the empty street.

Sammy said, "Hey, what are we looking for, anyway?"

Kathy kept staring out the window. "I thought I saw a strange car. It scared me."

Sammy said, "Hah! You're as easy to scare as a mouse, Kathy. I don't see how you live through Halloween."

Bill said, "Don't let Sammy bug you, Kathy. What did the car look like?"

She said, "Gray. A dent in the fender. Four doors. Driving slow.

"And the two men in it were wearing

silver-mirror sunglasses ... you know, the kind that make you look like you're a space alien ... without real eyes."

Sammy said, "What's so strange about that? Lots of people wear them.

"And I bet there are a thousand gray dented cars!

"A million!

"A billion!

"A trillion!

"A quadrillion!

"A quintil ... "

Bill stopped him. "Hold it, Sammy. Let me guess. You learned the number periods in school this week? That's great, but let Kathy talk."

Kathy went on. "Well, I wouldn't have paid any attention, except I think it went by yesterday, too."

Dave headed toward the phone. "Then we should call the police."

Mrs. Tandy said, "I don't think you'll have to. Look in the driveway. Isn't that Rita Sanchez?"

A small young woman dressed in jeans stepped out of a car.

The car drove off and she knocked on the door of the house.

Sammy was there in a second.

He threw it open.

He said, "I know you.

"You're a policeman ... er ... police lady ... er ... police officer."

Officer Sanchez laughed. "How do you know me?"

Sammy said, "You talked to our class about bike safety last year."

Officer Sanchez said, "Do you remember anything from the class?"

Sammy nodded. "I remember I should make hand signals when I turn. And I remember how pretty you are ... a lot prettier than Chief Hemster!

"So can you sit down and have some French toast with us?"

Bill said, "That's a good idea. And besides, Officer Sanchez, I think Kathy has something to tell you."

So while they ate, Kathy told her about the men and the car.

Officer Sanchez said, "I'll keep my eyes open for them today. Maybe they ARE connected to the burglaries.

"After all, Halloween would be a good night for them to get a close look into people's houses. All they'd have to do is put on costumes and ring bells.

"Everyone in town dresses up in costume, even grown-ups. No one would notice a burglar.

"I'll be in costume myself. In fact, I have to rig one up."

Kathy said shyly, "Would you like me to get one ready for you, Officer Sanchez? We are making ours. I could do yours at the same time."

Officer Sanchez smiled. "That would be a big help. But you'll all have to call me Rita for now.

"I don't want other people to find out I'm a police officer."

She stood up. "Thanks for breakfast! You sure are good cooks."

She waved and went out the door.

Then Mrs. Tandy asked Bill to help her get something up from the basement closet. They brought up two HUGE boxes, the kind that movers use.

They set them down on the dining-room floor.

"Here!" said Mrs. Tandy. "It's a Halloween surprise for you.

"Dig in, everybody!"

Chapter 6: Costumes!

Bill said, "What's in these boxes?"

Mrs. Tandy said, "Open one and spill it out."

Sammy grabbed a box and turned it

over. Out poured a landslide of clothes.

Mrs. Tandy said, "What do you think? Any good for costumes?"

Dave wheeled over. "They look WON-DERFUL! Let's go through them!"

Sammy said, "Rotten rats! I just re-membered! I have to finish my skeleton!

"I have to paint the other side ... right now ... or it won't be dry by to-night. But I sure wish I could help you with Rita's costume, Kathy."

Kathy said, "That's OK, Sammy. I'll help you paint first. It won't take us long to finish."

They went down to the basement.

Mrs. Tandy, Bill, and Dave pulled out clothes from the boxes. They laid them all over the chairs and table. The dining room looked like a flea market!

Besides clothes, there were dozens of scarves ... big squares of bright, silky cloth. Striped. Dotted. Flowered. Every kind of design.

Mrs. Tandy said, "I've saved every pretty scarf I ever had. They're worn-out, but they're beautiful colors."

Dave said, "When did you get all these clothes? And where? They don't all look your size."

Mrs. Tandy said, "I began saving them years ago ... but not for Halloween.

"I use them for making rugs ... like the rugs in Kathy's and Sammy's rooms.

"I save old, torn clothes and left-over cloth from sewing.

"And friends give me all their old things."

Dave said, "It's a real gold mine on Halloween!"

By then Kathy and Sammy were back from the basement.

Kathy pulled something from the pile.

"Oh, look at this black, shiny bath robe! The sleeves are big, like wings.

"I could go as a bat, Mrs. T.! I could put a black cloth on my head, and use a head band to keep it there.

"And it's warm enough today, I could wear my black sandals."

Mrs. Tandy said, "Great idea, Kathy!"

Dave pulled out a football shirt. He said, "Bill, can I borrow your helmet? I'll be a football hero."

Kathy smiled. "Your arms are so strong from wheeling your chair, you LOOK like a football hero."

Sammy sang out, "Kathy likes Da-a-ave! Kathy likes Da-a-a-ve!"

Kathy turned bright red.

Bill poked Sammy and whispered, "How can you tease Kathy like that? She's always so nice to you!"

Sammy poked him back and said,

"Don't worry, she likes it. She's just too shy to tell Dave herself."

Mrs. Tandy said, "Let's come up with an idea for your costume, Bill.

"Anything look good to you?"

Bill said, "That red bandana."

Sammy jumped. "Red banana? Where?"

Bill said, "Not baNANa. A banDANa! With a D! A bandana is a scarf, like cowboys wear. I could be a cowboy!

53

No, a rodeo clown!"

Kathy said, "I remember the clown at the rodeo! He was wearing cut-offs and knee socks.

"And had about twenty scarves hanging from his belt."

Bill started digging through the pile of scarves.

Mrs. Tandy said, "Now what are you planning for Officer San ... er, um, for Rita's costume, Kathy?"

Kathy pointed. "What about that old white jumpsuit?

"Wouldn't it make a good space suit?"

Mrs. Tandy said, "Wonderful! And I even have an old bike helmet she could use."

Dave said, "That would be perfect. And look at the big pockets in the jumpsuit. She could keep her police stuff in them."

Just then, Mop woke up from a nap under the dining-room table.

He started sniffing at an old shirt on a chair.

Sammy laughed. "Mop wants a costume, too! Let's make him one!"

They found a little white sailor shirt that one of the neighbor's children had grown out of long ago.

The collar was blue, with red stars on the corners.

Sammy put it on Mop and buttoned it up the front.

Mop trotted around the room. Then he grabbed a red tie that was hanging down from the table and ran.

Mrs. Tandy said, "Maybe he'd like that around his neck. Get his clothes for me and I'll iron them."

They chased after Mop and got the shirt and tie from him.

Sammy said, "We all have to iron our costumes, except me. So I'll iron Rita's things."

Just then the doorbell rang.

Sammy ran to open it.

There stood a strange man ... a man wearing silver-mirror sunglasses!

Chapter 7:
Ghosts and Scarecrows

The man smiled at Sammy and stepped into the house without being asked.

He said, "Hello, my little man.

"May I have a minute of your time?"

He spoke through his nose ... in a too-smooth, too-friendly voice.

Bill heard it, too. He walked up to Sammy's side.

Dave quickly joined them at the doorway and asked, "What can we do for you?"

The man said, "I'm with the People Against Pollution. PAP. Here is my permit from the police."

Dave looked at it and said, "I haven't heard of your group before."

The man said, "We are a little-known pollution group, but a fine one. I have a flyer for you to read. It tells all about the work our group does.

"Now you just look it over while I wait. I'll just stand here and answer any questions about pollution.

"Then you can think it over. I'll come around again in a few days. I'll take your donations then."

He handed a folder to Bill.

Bill said, "We are busy with something right now. I won't be able to read it while you wait."

The man backed away and said, "Well, thanks for your time, gentlemen."

He turned and left.

The minute he was gone Kathy said, "Boy, do I have something to tell you! I'm so glad he stopped here. That's one of the men from the gray car!

"He seems like he has a good reason for being in the neighborhood. They aren't robbers, after all ... I guess."

Sammy said, "Well, he may not be a robber, but I didn't like him.

"Calling me 'my little man' and calling us 'gentlemen' and that stuff! And besides, that seems like a pretty dumb way to collect money.

"Why didn't he ask for donations right away?"

Dave said, "I didn't like him, either. I don't like people who step into the house without being invited."

Bill put down the folder.

He said, "We can look at this thing later. Right now let's fix up the outside of the house."

So they all got to work.

Sammy brought up one of his horrible spiders from the basement.

He hung it on the front porch and said, "We need this up here!"

Bill said, "That's GREAT, Sammy. It will scare the WITS out of the trick-or-treaters."

Sammy pointed across the yard. "Look at what Dave and Kathy are doing!"

They had an old white sheet.

They tied a bunch of rags into the center, to make a ghost's head.

The rest of the sheet hung down all around it.

Kathy drew big eyes on the head with a black marking pen.

Then she tied a long, thin rope to the top of the head.

She fastened a rock to the end of the rope.

A branch of an oak tree stuck out over the driveway.

Dave called, "Give us a hand with this, will you, Bill? We need to get this rope over that tree branch!

"Can you throw the rock that high?"

Bill threw the rock in the air with all his might.

It flew over the branch, trailing the rope after it.

Kathy took the rope off the rock. Pulling the rope with her, she ran into the woods.

She called, "Watch what happens when I pull the rope!"

The ghost began to dance up and down above the driveway.

Mrs. Tandy said, "GREAT! It's perfectly wonderful!"

Kathy said, "I'll pull it up into the air. Then I'll tie the rope to a tree until we want to make it move again."

Sammy loved it. "It's AWEsome! Can I work it later? I could come out here between five and six tonight. That's when the little kids come around.

"Holy cow!" he added. "What time is it now?"

Dave said, "Just noon."

Bill grabbed his bike off the porch. "We've got to hurry things up. Mr. Reed said our invitations would be ready by twelve. I'll get them. Back in a flash!"

Mrs. Tandy went to a dark corner of the garage. She brought out some huge cornstalks.

She said, "I passed a farm stand yesterday morning and bought these. I

thought you might like them!"

Sammy said, "They're PERFECT! Let's stand them up and make corn shocks. I'll tie them together at the top."

When the corn shocks were tied, Dave

said, "Let's put our pumpkins on the grass in front of them."

Kathy said, "Oh, no! We haven't even carved the pumpkins yet!

"And we still have to hand out the in-vitations!"

Her thin little face looked so worried, Sammy began to laugh.

He said, "Kathy! You look like a scared mouse again! You worry about everything!"

Kathy smiled. She said, "Maybe I DO worry a lot.

"But I was hoping to make a scarecrow, too, to stand near the corn shocks. Do you think we can do it all before five?"

Sammy said, "Sure. Let's make the scarecrow right now.

"We can dress him in old clothes from the box.

"We can make his head out of a bag stuffed with newspapers. Let's go!"

When Bill came back he saw TWO scarecrows near the corn shocks.

As he rode up the driveway a ghost came flying down on him.

Horrible sounds came out of the woods.

He jammed on his brakes.

He yelled, "All RIGHT! It's GREAT!

"Now get out your black haunted houses, Sammy. We can glue these invitations onto them right now."

Sammy said, "HOUSES! I haven't cut them out yet! I forgot!

"Kathy, it's your fault. You should have worried about something that's REALLY important. ME!"

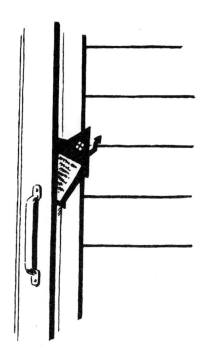

Chapter 8:
The Stolen Invitation

They couldn't help smiling.

This time SAMMY looked like the worried mouse.

His eyebrows pulled together.

His mouth turned down.

His hair stuck out.

Bill laughed and hugged him. He said, "No problem. We all can help cut out the houses."

Kathy said, "Let's cut them three at a time. We can finish fast!"

They raced into the house.

Kathy found a glue stick.

Sammy hunted up some black paper.

Mrs. Tandy and Bill got out five pairs of scissors.

Dave made some sandwiches for a quick lunch. They gobbled them down with milk and began cutting.

Dave said, "I'm not that good at using scissors ... I'll glue."

They finished the invitations in a hurry. Soon they were ready to go around and hand them out.

Then Officer Sanchez called through

the door, "Anyone home?"

Sammy opened it. "Come in, Rita! Come right in!

"Want some cold water? Pop?

"Milk? Want a cookie?"

They sat her down.

She said, "I can only stay a minute.

"I just wanted to keep you up-to-date. I haven't seen the gray car that was worrying you."

Bill said, "Well, we have. One of the guys in the gray car came inside our house. He said they were working against pollution.

"They have a permit to go around to all the houses in town. They're handing out these folders."

Officer Sanchez said, "He came to your house? Hmm ... well, I haven't seen them yet. I guess they haven't been to the blocks I was checking.

"I worked one street north of here, in both directions."

Sammy said, "Well, they might be going there tomorrow. Maybe they're just working on this street today.

"Oh, I almost forgot. I want to show you something!"

He ran out and came back with the space suit.

He said, "I ironed it for you myself. Here, try it on."

She had it on in a minute.

Sammy said, "It's a winner!

"You'll look EXACTLY like you're going into space!"

Bill asked, "Can you go trick-or-treating with us tonight?"

She smiled and said, "Why, I believe I will! That way I can keep an eye on things ... and feel like a kid again.

"What time are you going?"

Dave said, "Seven o'clock. Right after our haunted house is over."

Officer Sanchez took off the costume.

She said, "Well, I'm going back outside now. Suppose I meet you here at six forty-five."

Then she left.

The Woodlanders went to pass out their invitations. They started at one end of their own street, which was two blocks long.

They knew every person who lived on their block.

Every house except the Tolskys' had kids living in it.

Sammy said, "Maybe Mr. and Mrs. Tolsky will come. They like kids, even though they don't have any."

When they rang the bell, no one was home. So they put an invitation inside the screen door.

Then they went to the other block on their street.

It was a long, curvy one.

Finally they had only two houses left. They walked around the last curve.

Sammy pointed. "Look, Kathy! There are the pollution people!"

The men were sitting in their car ... just sitting there.

Sammy said, "They must have worn

themselves out. But they didn't have all that many houses to go to."

Mrs. Tandy said, "They must be wimps! Why, we went up to all the houses on these two blocks. It took us less than half an hour.

"Those two have been around here half the day!"

Dave was a little worried about them. He whispered to the others, "If you ask me, they're up to no good!"

They knocked on the door of the last

house. No one answered. They put the invitation inside the screen door.

Sammy shouted, "Hooray! All done! Now we can go carve our pumpkins!"

■   ■   ■

They didn't see what one of the men did after they left.

He went up to the house.

He opened the screen door.

He picked up the invitation and read it.

He carried it to the car and showed it to the other man.

He said, "I guess a lot of people will be away from home tonight."

Then, smiling widely, he stuffed it into his pocket.

Chapter 9: Pumpkin Heads

Five big pumpkins sat on the kitchen table.

Everybody chose a kitchen knife for carving.

Bill said, "Remember, everyone, be sure you take a knife with a thick wooden handle that's easy to hold."

Sammy made a face. "Boy, I remember what happened to Bill last year!"

Dave said, "What?"

Bill said, "I picked up a knife with a thin, smooth steel handle. On my FIRST cut into the pumpkin, my hand slid down onto the blade.

"Kathy grabbed my hand to make the bleeding slow down.

"I ended up in the hospital, getting sewn up. See?"

He showed Dave and Mrs. Tandy the scar on his palm.

Sammy said, "I like making scary pumpkins ... but not with drips of BLOOD!

"That was disGUSTing! So keep your blood inside your skin this time!"

They started to work on their pumpkins.   First they cut circles around the
stems.

Then they lifted the tops off.

Sammy said, "Yuck!   Look at those
slippery strings sticking to them.

"This is the part I HATE ... taking out
the pumpkin guts."

They reached inside and pulled out
wet, pulpy strings.   The seeds hung to the
pulp.

Their arms got slimy.

Their nails filled up with pumpkin pulp.

Then the juice started to dry on their arms. Their skin began to feel tight.

Mrs. Tandy said, "It's a mess, but it's FUN to be messy ... well, for a little while at least!

"Now, don't forget to save all the seeds. Here, put them in this."

She placed a big bowl in the middle of the table.

She said, "We have to clean them ... and salt them ... and roast them for an hour."

Kathy said, "I love them, all brown and munchy." She set the oven to 250 degrees.

They took turns washing the pulp off the seeds.

Kathy put them into a buttered pan. She shook some salt onto them.

Bill put the pan into the oven.

Then they got back to carving.

Bill gave his pumpkin two different-sized round eyes.

Sammy's pumpkin had one square eye and one triangle eye.

Mrs. Tandy cut two big triangles, only partway through the skin. Then she put a prune in the center of each.

Dave looked around and said, "OK! I can see these are going to be great jack-o'-lanterns. So let's have prizes!

"A candy bar for the scariest-looking pumpkin.

"One for the happiest-looking pumpkin.

"And one for the most different-looking pumpkin.

"Now let's go!"

Dave wasn't carving his pumpkin at all. He was sticking things onto it with nails instead.

He took two small apples out of the cupboard.

He stuck nails into the pumpkin where the eyes belonged.

He stuck apples onto the nails.

He stuck on a carrot for the nose.

Then he started on the mouth. He glued on pumpkin-seed teeth and red rug-yarn lips.

Kathy said, "Yours is great, Dave! You'll get the prize for the most different-looking pumpkin!"

The others kept on carving, but they kept watching Dave.

One by one they began adding things to their pumpkins.

Sammy got a big piece of cotton.

He glued it onto his pumpkin's lip and chin. He dug a hole where the nose would be. He stuck a big red radish in the hole.

He said, "How do you like it?"

Bill laughed. "It looks just like Santa Claus! It's a Sant-o'-lantern!"

Then Bill looked at Mrs. Tandy's pumpkin. She had it covered with a big white dish towel.

She said, "You don't get to see it until you're all done with yours."

Just then Sammy let out a yelp.

Bill ran around the table to him. "What's wrong, Sammy?"

He looked at Sammy's pumpkin. There was BLOOD on it! Blood on its cheek! Blood on the cotton on its lip!

Blood dripping onto its beard!

Bill said, "Holy cow! Let me see where you cut yourself!"

Sammy said, "Calm down, calm down. I didn't cut myself. What do you think ... I'm a pumpkin head like you?

"I've just got a nosebleed again. I'll fix it."

He pulled off a puff of cotton from his pumpkin's beard.

He stuffed it into his nose.

Kathy ran for an ice cube.

She wrapped it in a dish towel and

held it to the top of his nose.

Mrs. Tandy ran for a wash rag.

Sammy wiped off the blood that had run down his lip.

Bill said, "I'll get you some fresh cotton, Sammy. We can clean up your pumpkin."

Sammy said, "No, sir! You leave my pumpkin alone! I changed my mind about the blood. It's the perfect finishing touch.

"I'm entering my pumpkin just the way it is! Blood-beard the Pirate!

"He will win the scariest pumpkin prize, wait and see."

Chapter 10:
Planning the Scavenger Hunt

At last, five grinning pumpkins sat waiting.

It was easy to pick winners.

Dave's was the most different by far. He

had added two yellow peppers to make big ears. So he kept one candy bar.

To her pumpkin, Mrs. Tandy had simply added a giant grin. No nose. No ears. No hair. Just triangle eyes and a great big grin.

It easily won the candy bar for being the happiest.

And Sammy's took the prize for being the scariest.

He said, "Maybe I'll get lucky and have a nosebleed every Halloween! Thanks for the candy!"

Then Bill said, "Oh, no! We forgot to make the popcorn balls! And the lemonade!"

Mrs. Tandy started right in squeezing lemons.

Kathy and Dave started making popcorn with the electric popper.

Finally they had eight big brown bags full of it. It was plenty for making the popcorn balls!

Then they mixed sugar into the lemon juice.

Mrs. Tandy said, "We can add water to it when the people come."

Then she said, "Oh, for gosh sakes!"

Dave said, "NOW what's wrong?"

She said, "We haven't made the scavenger hunt lists!

"And we only have an hour before the little kids start coming around. And we need about fifteen copies."

So they sat down in a hurry. Bill handed out pencils. He gave them each three pieces of paper.

Kathy said, "The hunt I was on, there were about twenty things to find."

Sammy asked, "What kinds of things? Do you remember?"

Kathy answered, "Uh ... let me see. Well, I remember one thing was a big red button."

Bill said, "That sounds easy enough. I bet we have every color button there is in our button box. Let's write a big red button down for the first thing."

Kathy said, "Another thing we had to find was a soup bone. Only two groups found that. One of the bones had been dug up by a dog."

Sammy said, "Good! A soup bone's hard to find. Let's write that down too."

Kathy said, "We had to bring back a bug ... and a pickle ... and a dog collar.

"That's all I can remember, though."

They wrote those down.

Dave said, "OK, now we add our own. How about a leaf, an oak leaf ... a blue shoe ... and three safety pins."

Mrs. Tandy added, "We could have them try for a pink hair ribbon ... and a mousetrap!"

Sammy said, "How about a light bulb ... no, someone might break it ... that's too dangerous."

Bill said, "Well, then, how about some paper and plastic things, like a bubble-gum wrapper ... and a magazine four months old ... and an egg carton."

Kathy nodded. "Those are great ones. Hey, do you think anyone could find a valentine left over from last February? Let's add that!"

Then Sammy grinned. He said, "BILL sure could find one! He saved one Annie Lee sent him. She's his dream girl!"

Bill said, "Yep, she is."

Sammy said, "Yep? Is that all you're going to say ... yep? You mean you're not going to get mad at me for teasing you?"

90

Bill said, "Nope. You reminded me about my valentine. Now if we go on the hunt, I'll be able to use it!"

Kathy asked, "Do you think it would be fair if we go on the scavenger hunt ourselves, as a team?

"I'd love to do it!"

Bill said, "Sure. It'll be fun. We just won't get any prizes."

Dave said, "Come on, let's finish the lists!"

So they thought of ...

> a soup can
> a green sock
> a 1988 penny
> a two-colored marble
> a map of Europe
> a shower-curtain ring
> a peach
> a red ball-point pen
> ... and a milk carton.

Sammy said, "THERE! Done! I bet that's more than twenty. Now let's get our costumes on.

"You have to get ready to answer the door. The little guys will be coming around trick-or-treating.

"And I have to get out to the woods FAST!

"It's time to fly the ghost around and make horrible noises!

"Halloween's here!

"And we are ready for it at last!"

Kathy went to put on her Halloween costume.

But something had been bothering her all afternoon ... the thought of the men in the parked car.

Then it hit her.

She went flying through the house back to the others.

She told them, "Something about those men in the gray car is WRONG!"

Sammy said, "There you go, worrying again. And it's late. You should be putting on your costume!"

But Dave said, "Just a minute. What is it, Kathy?"

Kathy said, "For one thing ... those sunglasses!

"They didn't need them. They weren't even parked facing the sun.

"What if they were wearing them to hide their faces ... so a police officer wouldn't know them?"

Dave said, "That could be, Kathy. And something else still bugs me. I keep thinking the man who came into our house just wanted a look around."

Mrs. Tandy said, "So you think the strangers really might be the burglars!"

Dave said, "Well, it does seem funny when you add it all together. I'll phone Chief Hemster."

Bill said, "We should all be on the lookout for trouble tonight."

Chapter 11:
Space Creatures

They hurried into their costumes.

Mrs. Tandy helped Bill put on make-up for his rodeo-clown face.

Kathy drew black and blue marks on

Dave's football-hero face.

Then Sammy turned off all the lights.
He shouted, "Look at me!

"I'm GREAT!"

He danced around in front of the mirror in his leaf bag.

His glowing skeleton jumped around in the dark.

In a minute he was running outside to start the awful-sounds tape.

Bill called after him. "Wait! Why do you have a squirt gun and that bucket, Sammy?"

Sammy called back, "In case a ghost tries to get me!"

He ran to the rope in the woods and took hold of it.

The little kids began to show up.

There were vampires. Sailors. Ghosts. Dolls.

There were figures out of books and

comics.   The Wizard of Oz.   Charlie Brown.   A giant spider.

Eight children arrived together, dressed as Snow White and the Seven Dwarfs.

Sammy made the ghost in the tree jump down at everyone.

He played his tape of awful noises.

Trick-or-treaters ran screaming and laughing to the front door.

Almost every one of them carried a pillowcase or a shopping bag.

But one little boy had a small plastic pumpkin for his treats. They kept spilling out.

Bill got him a shopping bag.

At 6:00 Sammy rushed inside.

It was time for the haunted house to open.

People felt their way through the basement, along the glowing rope. Parents. Teens. Grade schoolers.

Wet, stringy rags hit faces.

"YUCK!"

"HELP!"

"ICK!"

Spidery shadows sprang to life under Sammy's quick-moving flashlight.

"OH! LOOK OUT!"

Bump! Thump! Bang!

"Oops, that's a chair."

"ISH! What's this you're giving me? Do I have to eat it?"

Sammy's worst monster voice thundered, "It's only a worm."

And finally, there was the sound of people talking and laughing and munching cookies.

At 6:50, Chief Hemster finally arrived.

Mrs. Tandy, the friendly ape, fed him cookies and lemonade.

By this time the other guests had left on the scavenger hunt.

Sammy said, "Looks like that's about it." He went to the back of the basement to lock the outside door.

Then they heard him call, "Oops, here come some more!"

Two people walked in.

The next minute Sammy shouted, "Everybody! Chief! Come here! Fast!"

Then he said, "Don't make a move, you two. We've got you now!"

He shined his light in their faces.

There stood two space creatures. They wore purple suits with hoods, trimmed in silver foil.

Feelers stuck out of the tops of their heads.

Their faces and hands were all green.

And they were wearing SILVER-MIRROR SUNGLASSES!

In his meanest voice Sammy boomed, "OK! The game's up! Take off those glasses. We know you guys!"

One of the space creatures said, "Of

course you know us, Sammy."

They took off their glasses.

It was Mr. and Mrs. Tolsky!

Mrs. Tolsky said, "Can't we come through the haunted house? We got your nice invitation. What's wrong? Are we too late?"

Sammy couldn't answer! He felt like hiding.

All he could do was stand there, red-faced under his skeleton mask.

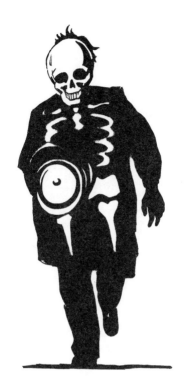

Chapter 12:
The Real Burglars

Just then Rita walked in the basement door.

She said, "Sorry I'm a bit late. I'll run and put my costume on."

The chief said, "Yes, we need you on the lookout.

"For a minute we thought Sammy had caught the burglars.

"It turned out they were just two space creatures from down the block.

"Any sign of the men or the car?"

Rita said, "No, I've only seen ghosts and goblins."

The chief left. Rita went to get into her costume.

Mrs. Tandy said, "You know, I think I'll skip the trick-or-treating and scavenger hunting."

Sammy said, "Why, Mrs. T.?"

Mrs. Tandy said, "Well, around now, the older kids will be trick-or-treating.

"If I'm here I can give out the rest of our popcorn balls.

"Besides, someone should be here when the scavenger hunters come back!"

Sammy said, "But you'll miss all the fun!"

Mrs. Tandy said, "Why, bless your heart, Sammy, I don't mind.

"I'll get to see their costumes, and they'll get to see a gorilla. Besides, you'll only be gone an hour!"

Sammy hugged her. "OK, then. But don't be scared. I'll hurry back."

He grabbed Bill by both arms and roared, "The trick-or-treat-scavenger-skeleton has you in his power. So come with me!"

They ran to get four pillowcases, plus one for Rita. Then they all hurried out the door into the dark night.

They started at a house a few blocks away. Then they began to work their way toward home.

By 7:50 they had been to nearly sixty houses.

105

They had found only six things from their scavenger list ... but their pillowcases were heavy with treats.

Sammy stopped to count his riches.

"I have sixty-seven candy bars," he bragged.

"Some of the houses gave out more than one to each person.

"And I have three packages of home-made fudge. And three apples.

"And here are five popcorn balls. And three HUGE home-made cookies.

"If I'm really careful, it will last until December. Then I'll get more candy during the holidays."

Bill said, "Your Halloween candy never lasts until December. Last year it was gone in four weeks.

"And then MY candy disappeared, too. It's a real mystery."

Sammy didn't answer. He just grinned

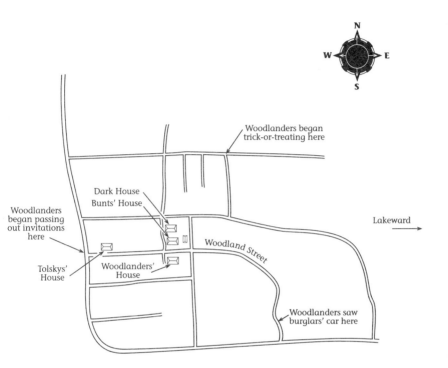

N
W   E
S

Woodlanders began
trick-or-treating here

Dark House
Bunts' House

Woodlanders
began passing
out invitations
here

Tolskys'
House

Woodlanders'
House

Woodland Street

Lakeward

Woodlanders saw
burglars' car here

under his skeleton mask.

Then Dave said, "Come on, guys. Time to go home. We only have five minutes before the scavengers get back."

Kathy pointed to a house that had no lights on.

107

She said, "Look, Rita, the Bunts' house is on the other side of this dark house. We can go up this driveway, and down the Bunts' driveway.

"Then we end up on our block. The Bunts let us do it all the time."

They got to the back of the Bunts' lot.

Suddenly they heard footsteps heading their way. Sammy's flashlight shined on two people.

They had on store-bought Halloween costumes. One was a lizard and the other was a dog.

They were big. High-school-sized.

Rita said, "Hi, kids! The lights are out at the next house. No one's home. No use stopping there ... or are you just cutting through, too?"

The dog answered in a growl, "Just cutting through." He waved some empty pillowcases and kept walking.

Dave whispered, "I wonder if he goes to Bluff Lake High ... I've heard that voice before."

The Woodlanders led Rita down the Bunts' long driveway. Then they ran down to their own house.

The scavenger hunters were there,

109

ready to pick the winner.

Mrs. Tandy had checked all the things the teams had brought in.

Then Sammy had a sudden terrible thought. He whispered to her, "Holy hot dogs! We forgot to get prizes for them!"

Mrs. Tandy whispered, "It's OK. I thought of that a minute ago. I've got prizes, from the freezer."

First prize was a home-baked chocolate cake.

Second was a home-baked apple pie.

Third was a half-dozen home-baked cupcakes.

In less than a minute the scavenger hunters left.

Then Dave suddenly wheeled toward the door. He shouted, "Rita! Woodlanders! Come on! Let's get out of here!

"Something else has been going round and round in my mind. I just figured it out! Come on!"

Kathy said, "What's wrong? Where are we going?"

Dave said, "Remember that lizard and the dog?

"Well, they couldn't be regular trick-or-treaters!

"For one thing their pillowcases were EMPTY!

"And I'll tell you why! Those pillowcases were for carrying away stolen stuff! They were there to break in!

"Now I know that voice. It was the

111

man who came to our house!

"They are the BURGLARS! COME ON!"

But Rita said, "Don't try to go after them. I'll meet the chief there. You have to stay here.

"They might be armed.

"I promise to get back here as soon as we nab them. I'll tell you everything then. But you have to promise not to go near that dark house.

"Now, promise?"

Five voices said, "I promise."

Rita radioed Chief Hemster.

They heard her say, "What? There's been one burglary already? And on this street? Well, I'm afraid there's more trouble in the air. I'll pick you up."

Rita ran out.

A minute later Bill exclaimed, "Hey, where's Sammy? SAMMY!"

Everyone ran around looking for him.

Bill shouted, "Come out, Sammy. Stop scaring us. We know you're here."

But no one answered.

Sammy was GONE!

Chapter 13: Gotcha!

"Gone?" Mrs. Tandy said. "He can't be gone!"

Dave said, "You don't think he would break his promise ... and sneak over to the dark house?"

Bill shook his head. "No. If he gives his word, he keeps it.

"He's the world's biggest pest, but he doesn't break promises."

Mrs. Tandy said, "We should get in the car and look for him."

Dave shouted, "CAR! Sammy could have kept his promise not to go to the house. But he could have gone looking for the burglars' car!"

Kathy said, "What if he finds it? What if the police don't catch the robbers in time? What if they go back to their car and they find Sammy there?"

Mrs. Tandy said, "And if they have a gun ... "

Bill said, "How about looking where we saw it parked today? That wasn't far from the Bunts' house!"

They raced out to the station wagon.

Dave threw himself into the driver's seat. Bill quickly put the wheelchair into the back.

They drove down the street.

As soon as they went around the bend, they spotted the gray car.

Dave parked, and they sneaked over.

Mrs. Tandy whispered, "LOOK! There's a rope all around the car! A rope tied to every door handle!"

Bill whispered, "SAMMY did that! And I bet he's hiding near here!"

"He would wait to see them try to get into it.

"We have to find him and get away from here!"

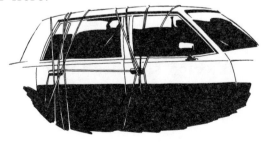

117

Dave wheeled up the driveway.

The others hurried after him.

Suddenly Kathy grabbed Bill's arm.

She pointed and whispered, "Look there! I bet that's Sammy!"

Something was moving in the bushes along the driveway.

Bill made a flying grab.

He said, "Gotcha, you silly little goose!"

They heard a mean voice hiss, "Get your hands off me, kid, or you'll get hurt, BAD!"

Dave hurried forward.

He threw himself out of his chair toward the voice.

At the same moment a Sammy-tornado flew out from behind another bush.

The three boys pushed the man to the ground. He landed flat on his back.

Sammy shouted, "YOU'RE NOT GOING

118

TO HURT MY BROTHER!" He sat down on the man's stomach. He took a good look. It was the man in the dog mask.

The man groaned, "Stop jiggling! I give up! You're mashing my guts out!"

Sammy growled, "Then stop trying to get away!"

The man gasped, "I'm just a trick-or-treater, on the way to my car."

Bill looked in the bushes. He saw a big pillowcase with a radio and some silverware spilling out of it.

Then a police car drove up.

Out stepped Rita Sanchez, still dressed in her space suit.

Behind her was Chief Hemster.

A third officer led the lizard out of the police car in handcuffs.

Officer Sanchez said, "We caught him red-handed.

"Every room in that house looked like

a tornado hit it.

"Clothes everywhere.

"Drawers half-open.

"Magazines and towels all over the floor."

The lizard grunted. "It was that way when we went in. We hardly even got started in there.

"We couldn't find anything, it was such a mess.

"We kept tripping over damp towels on the floor.

"We thought some creep had been in before us to rob the joint.

"That's why my partner went to get the car. He got disgusted. All we could find in that pig pen was the silverware and one lousy radio.

"That was the messiest house I ever ran across!"

Officer Sanchez said, "That's the first

time I've heard a criminal place a complaint against a victim."

The dog sneered, "This is a hot one, getting arrested by someone in a space suit. They'll throw the case right out of court."

Chief Hemster said, "Guess again, pal. This is one of our top officers!"

Then they took the burglars off to the police station.

It was 11:00 at night.

The Woodlanders had cleaned up from the party.

They were headed for bed when the doorbell rang.

Three voices yelled, "TRICK-OR-TREAT!"

Mop began to race in circles.

Sammy ran to the window.

There stood Chief Hemster with Officer Sanchez and the other officer.

A few minutes later they were all munching Halloween candy and oatmeal cookies.

Mop had candy corn stuck to his teeth. He was busy trying to scrape it off with his paw.

Sammy said, "Poor Mop. He doesn't know how to eat it. He only gets candy on special holidays.

"Well, this was the special-est holiday of all. In fact, this was my favorite Halloween ever.

"We made a haunted house.

"We had a scavenger hunt.

"We made a flying ghost.

"We made horrible noises in the woods.

"We went trick-or-treating.

"And we helped catch the crooks who were haunting the town."

Bill said, "You left out the greatest thing of all ... we might get into *The Guinness Book of Records*!

"We've just eaten half a pillowcase of candy. And Sammy, it was YOUR PILLOWCASE!

"Hah! Sammy, for once you didn't get my Halloween candy!"

Sammy just said, "That's OK, Bill old pal," and took a drink of milk.

Bill said, "Wait. Something's fishy. Why aren't you mad?"

He looked around the dining room.

"Just a minute, Sammy! Where's MY pillowcase full of candy? And Kathy's? And Dave's?

"We laid them right there on the sideboard when we came home! All three are gone!"

Sammy didn't say a word. He just sat there smiling, like the happiest Halloween pumpkin.